21st
Century
Skills Library

COOL ARTS CAREERS

SCRIPTWRITER

MATT MULLINS

CHERRY LAKE
Publishing

Published in the United States of America by
Cherry Lake Publishing, Ann Arbor, Michigan
www.cherrylakepublishing.com

Content Adviser
Kenneth Dancyger, MA, Professor, Kanbar Institute of Film and Television,
Tisch School of the Arts, New York University

Special thanks to Orit Schwartz, Artistic Director at The BendFilm Festival

Photo Credits
Cover and page 1, ©iStockphoto.com/quavondo; page 4, ©Black Rock Digital/
Shutterstock, Inc.; page 6, ©Levent Konuk/Shutterstock, Inc.; page 10, ©Yuri
Arcurs/Shutterstock, Inc.; page 13, ©John Spence/Shutterstock, Inc.; page 14,
©Radu Razvan/Shutterstock, Inc.; page 15, ©Seandeburca/Dreamstime.com;
page 16, ©sonya etchison/Shutterstock, Inc.; page 18, ©Godfer/Dreamstime.com;
page 19, ©imagebroker/Alamy; page 20, ©Rick Becker-leckrone/Dreamstime.com;
page 22 and page 25, ©Goodluz/Shutterstock, Inc.; page 26, ©Dmitriy Shironosov/
Shutterstock, Inc.; page 28, ©Allstar Picture Library/Alamy

Library of Congress Cataloging-in-Publication Data
Mullins, Matt.
   Scriptwriter/by Matt Mullins.
      p. cm.—(Cool arts careers)
   Includes bibliographical references and index.
   ISBN-13: 978-1-61080-135-5 (lib. bdg.)
   ISBN-10: 1-61080-135-0 (lib. bdg.)
   1. Motion picture authorship—Vocational guidance—Juvenile literature.
2. Television authorship—Vocational guidance—Juvenile literature. I. Title.
   PN1996.M835 2011
   808.2'3023—dc22   2011004781

Cherry Lake Publishing would like to acknowledge
the work of The Partnership for 21st Century Skills.
Please visit *www.21stcenturyskills*.org for more information.

Printed in the United States of America
Corporate Graphics Inc.
July 2011
CLFA09

COOL ARTS CAREERS

TABLE OF CONTENTS

CHAPTER ONE
SHOWING A STORY

Think of your favorite movie, television show, or video game. What did you love about the story? Have you ever thought about how the story was created?

Have you ever wondered who comes up with the stories for the videogames you play?

Stories for movies, TV shows, and video games come from the work of scriptwriters. Scriptwriters also write stage plays, Web site pages, informational videos, advertisements, and more. They create things for characters to say and situations for characters to deal with.

When actors or **directors** are interviewed, they often talk about writers. Every good film, play, or video begins with a **script**. A good script must include an interesting story, exciting action, and quality **dialogue**.

Writing for film or TV is different than writing for plays or radio. Film and TV require action and movement. Plays and radio programs focus more on dialogue. But all types of scripts share one important trait. Unlike novels, which can describe characters' thoughts, scripts must use action and dialogue to show what is going on in a character's mind. Scriptwriters need a good sense for movement and action. They use **images** to explain parts of stories without using dialogue.

Scripts also need good stories. Like a good book, if a movie or TV show doesn't have a story that pulls you in, you probably won't finish watching it. Scriptwriters who work on **drama** need a good ear for how people speak in real life. They need to understand how people's words affect their actions. They also need to know how to set up an interesting **conflict**. Many conflicts are based around characters who have different goals, such as a superhero and an evil villain. Other stories are about a single character with a problem to solve, such as a detective trying to discover who committed a crime.

Think about a **scene** where a boy named Frankie likes a girl named Kathy. Frankie sees Kathy at school. In a story or a novel, we may read that Frankie has a crush on Kathy. A writer may tell us how Frankie feels or describe the thoughts racing through Frankie's head when he passes Kathy in the hallway. The writer might also describe what Kathy is thinking or feeling. Scripts don't usually do that. In fact, most scripts wouldn't even tell us that Frankie has a crush on Kathy! Scripts show information instead of telling it. Here is a sample script.

Almost all movies and TV shows begin with a script.

INTERIOR SCHOOL HALLWAY — DAY

FRANKIE stands at his locker, talking with AARON about math homework. A group of four girls walks by, including KATHY, who carries a book and a folder. KATHY stops to talk with FRANKIE. The other girls pause briefly to look at her and FRANKIE, giggle, then move on. FRANKIE drops his books and folders into his locker loudly and then thrusts his hands into his pockets.

KATHY, cheerful, looks right at FRANKIE. FRANKIE drops his head.

                    KATHY
Hi, Frankie!

          FRANKIE, speaking quietly
Hi, Kathy.

                    KATHY
Frankie, Linda told me you helped her with her math problems after school yesterday.

FRANKIE stares at his feet and glances up nervously at KATHY.

                    FRANKIE
Yeah, we went over the algebra homework. It was hard, but not that hard. Linda didn't really need my help.

KATHY

Well, Linda said she didn't get it at all. She said you really helped her. I think you're sweet.

FRANKIE shuffles his feet, trying to appear absentminded, and shrugs his shoulders. He keeps his head down as he speaks.

FRANKIE

Aww. It was nothin', Kathy. Um, I'm sure you coulda helped her if you'd been around.

KATHY

Well, maybe you can help me sometime, too.

FRANKIE squirms.

FRANKIE

Naw. You wouldn't need my help.

FRANKIE suddenly looks up at Kathy and pulls his hands out of his pockets. He begins speaking quickly, a little more loudly.

FRANKIE

I mean, yes, of course I'd help you, Kathy! If you need it, I mean, if you think you, I mean, if you want to do homework. [Looks down again.] I mean, um . . .

How is this script different from a novel? First, we haven't read what Frankie feels. There is no narrator to explain the characters' feelings. Imagine how the script would look on a movie screen. When we see Frankie drop his chin and mumble, we can tell he's uncomfortable talking to Kathy. Maybe we see a hint of a smile on his face, too. Or maybe we see Frankie blush. From what the scriptwriter and film director show us, and how the actors use their voices and bodies, we can see that Frankie has a crush on Kathy. Scriptwriters give actors and directors what they need to show us a story.

LEARNING & INNOVATION SKILLS

There are many kinds of stories for scripts to tell. Comedy scripts will be funny or end happily. TV shows called situation comedies (or sitcoms) involve characters and places used throughout a series of shows. Dramas usually have more serious stories than comedies do. Some dramas are tragedies, which have unhappy endings. Other types of scripts include romances, mysteries, and fantasies. Do you have a favorite kind of story? Why is it your favorite?

CHAPTER TWO

A DAY ON THE JOB

Orit Schwartz worked on a television series called *Grounded for Life*. Orit was not a regular writer for the show, but she did write one episode.

Television writers often work closely with a group to create their scripts.

To write the episode, Orit joined the show's eight staff writers. "It's a cool job," said Orit, "because for the most part, you have some fun people you're working with. You're going to play."

Before she could start working on her script each day, she had to convince the producers and staff writers that she had a good idea. Many people pitch story ideas to a show's producers and writers. Producers listen to the ideas, then choose which story they want the team to work on.

Scriptwriters discuss the story and work out a **plot** together. Then the group assigns the actual writing to one or two writers. Orit worked with a cowriter on her script. The script was based on the idea of one young character getting her first car. The character had to study for her driver's license and take a driving test.

Every day, Orit would join the other writers, and they would talk, share jokes, and tell stories. This helped them come up with funny ideas to include in their scripts. Then she would get to writing. As she wrote, Orit discussed the script with her cowriter. Once they finished a **draft** of the script, they took it to the other writers.

Everyone read the script. Then they all talked about it. Writers pointed out which parts were funny and which didn't quite work. They would point out problems with the plot and suggest changes. Then Orit and her cowriter would rework the script based on the other writers' input. After they **revised** their first draft, the next step was a **table read**.

In a table read, writers listen carefully as actors sit around a table and read their parts. The director and the writers imagine what the action will look like as the actors perform. Scriptwriters listen for dialogue that is hard to understand. They also listen for lines that don't make sense or aren't very funny.

Then the scriptwriters revise their script again. On a TV show, directors have the cast run through the story. Actors read or speak their parts and move around on the **set** as directed. Some television shows also have dress rehearsals in front of live audiences. At these rehearsals and run-throughs, writers watch for problems so they can make further revisions as needed.

LEARNING & INNOVATION SKILLS

Orit Schwartz once wrote a short film. She and her film crew shot all the scenes in one day. Orit cast the film with actors she already knew. She also worked with a director, a cinematographer, and a small crew.

Short films are usually about 7 to 15 minutes long. Some are much shorter or longer. In a longer film, there is more time for the story to twist and turn. Characters can go through a lot of changes. How do you think a short script would need to be different from a longer one?

Table reads allow writers to hear what their dialogue sounds like spoken aloud.

13

Each TV script goes through many revisions before it is filmed. Writers sometimes even have to revise their scripts after they have started to be performed. The writer's job continues until the project is completely finished.

All types of writers must write and rewrite as they work. They throw away parts of their stories or change them to work better. Like other creative people, though, writers must stop working on a project at some point. Writing can almost always be improved, but writers must know when to let their script, essay, or book be done.

Revisions can sometimes be a long, difficult process.

Writers work closely with actors as they revise their scripts.

CHAPTER THREE
BECOMING A SCRIPTWRITER

Do you think you might want to become a scriptwriter one day? You can get started right now! Being a scriptwriter really only requires you to do two things: watch and write!

The more you write, the better your scripts will get.

Do you want to write screenplays for movies? Watch a lot of movies.

Do you want to write scripts for television shows? Watch a lot of television shows.

Do you want to write plays? Watch a lot of plays.

As you watch, try writing scripts of your own. Write movies, television stories, video game stories, or any other type of story. Borrow a video camera, get some friends together, and make a movie. Or gather a group of people to perform a play of your own.

21ST CENTURY CONTENT

New technology has made it easy to create videos of your own. Making movies used to require large, expensive cameras and a large film crew. Some movies still require all this, but others do not. A lot of people watch movies and short videos on their computers.

You can make your own movie with almost any video camera. Some people have even made movies with their phones. How would you show your movie to friends and family? Do you think you could you use the Internet to find a bigger audience for your movie?

You should also read a lot. Read anything you want to, whether it is a novel or a comic book. This will help you understand how to build plots, create interesting characters, and capture the audience's attention. The more you read and watch, the better you will understand what makes a good story.

There are many ways to break into the scriptwriting business. Some **screenwriters** start out in other careers. Some come from advertising, where they wrote ads for print and for radio and television. Others started out writing books. Some actors and newspaper writers have also become scriptwriters.

Reading is a great way to get new ideas for your scripts.

Some scriptwriters begin their careers writing for newspapers.

Scriptwriters also come from a variety of educational backgrounds. Some go to college and study writing, drama, or film. Others study marketing or advertising. Literature and history are also good topics to study.

Whatever subject you choose to study, you should always keep watching, reading, and writing. Go to film festivals. See a lot of movies in a short time, then think carefully about the stories.

Many film festivals have contests for young filmmakers. You could make a movie and enter it in one of these contests. Your film might even be shown in a theater.

Try making your own movies with friends.

Try to work on a movie set if you get a chance. Movies are shot all over the world, from small towns in Arizona to big cities such as Chicago. These movies often need people to fill the background in certain scenes. Instead of hiring professional actors, filmmakers fill these scenes with **extras**. Films advertise for extras in local newspapers and on TV programs. You could be an extra and see how a movie is made. This will help you become a better scriptwriter. You will remember what it was like to film a real movie scene and then be able to write your script like it was being filmed.

LIFE & CAREER SKILLS

It takes many people to turn a script into a movie or TV show. Scriptwriters must be flexible. Just as TV writers often work with other writers, they must also work with producers, directors, and film crews.

Some writers direct their scripts by themselves, but many allow other people to direct their scripts. If a prop breaks, the weather changes, or something else unexpected occurs, the script might need changes. The director might not like the way a scene is working and ask for it to be changed. In situations like these, a scriptwriter must revise parts of the script.

CHAPTER FOUR
SCRIPTWRITING IN THE FUTURE

Making movies and television will likely change a lot in the future, but writing scripts might not change much at all.

Today, we can watch movies and TV shows on our computers, on our phones, or in our cars. We can also

Handheld devices allow us to watch videos wherever we go.

watch them on television or at a movie theater. We can listen to radio programs and podcasts just about anywhere on portable devices or home stereos. In the future, we will likely have even more options for how we choose to enjoy our favorite movies and shows.

No matter how much technology changes, all of these movies and shows will still need skilled writers to create the scripts they are made from. Whether a script is made into a traditional stage play or a streaming Internet video, it will still need all the basic features of a good story. It will need interesting characters, a strong plot, and realistic dialogue.

 LIFE & CAREER SKILLS

There are many uses for scripts. Advertisements use scripts. Video games use scripts. Scriptwriters write video scripts that explain something a new company does. There are public service announcements—scripted advertisements for nonprofit organizations that help people in need. What scripts have you heard or seen performed in the last week? Where were you when you heard it or saw it? Did you hear it on the radio, on TV, in a theater, or in a mall? What other places have you heard the work of a scriptwriter? What kind of scripts would you like to write?

While some writers will continue to use pens and paper or a typewriter to create their scripts, others will take advantage of new technology. Special computer software can make it easier for scriptwriters to create properly formatted scripts. Small handheld computers allow them to write down ideas no matter where they are. Some writers even type their stories into cell phones.

As the world changes, people will want stories that reflect the times they live in. Being familiar with current events, modern slang, and what people are interested in will always be a useful skill for scriptwriters. Staying familiar with the changing culture allows writers to make sure their scripts are realistic and meaningful to audiences.

It is also important to pay attention to which kinds of stories are popular. This will help you stay competitive with other scriptwriters. Keep track of which shows and movies are most successful, and make note of what sets them apart from less successful ones.

While there will always be demand for good scriptwriters, it is a highly competitive field. You will need to be among the very best if you want to write full-time. Scriptwriters' pay varies widely, depending on how successful they are. Scriptwriters must also be prepared to go for long periods without work. Many will have to work other jobs in between writing assignments. Luckier writers might secure jobs as staff writers for TV shows or sign a long-term contract with a movie studio.

Tablet computers allow writers to work on their scripts and keep up with the latest news about shows and movies.

Getting jobs often requires scriptwriters to look for new opportunities constantly.

Networking is a very important skill to have. For many scriptwriters, the most difficult part of finding work is simply getting their feet in the door. There are so many people who want to write scripts for movies and TV shows that it can be difficult to stand out. The more people you know in the entertainment industry, the easier it will be to find a job.

Networking is an important skill for any career.

No matter how technology and culture change, though, there will always be a need for great stories. Keep reading, watching, and writing. Revise your work, and ask for opinions from your friends and family. Keep at it, and maybe one day you will see your characters up on the big screen speaking the lines you wrote!

21ST CENTURY CONTENT

In Japan, if you want to read some of the best-selling novels, you can only do it on your phone! Mobile phone novels are written with text messages. Scriptwriters must be able to take writing skills to whatever format is required.

Scriptwriters also work on multiple platforms. People who make movies set up Web sites with extra videos not shown in the movie. Sometimes they make short movies for cell phones. New technologies present new ways to watch or hear scripts.

Spike Lee has written and directed several award-winning films.

SOME FAMOUS
SCRIPTWRITERS

Steven Bochco (1943–) wrote for a number of successful and influential television series. *Hill Street Blues* (1981–1987) introduced multiple storylines to single television episodes. Its complex stories and characters challenged viewers in ways television never had before, and influence TV writing to this day.

Robert Bolt (1924–1995) wrote plays and screenplays. His work on the films *Lawrence of Arabia* (1962), *Doctor Zhivago* (1965), and *The Mission* (1986) earned him recognition as one of the most accomplished scriptwriters ever.

Diablo Cody (1978–) won an Academy Award for her screenplay for the movie *Juno* (2007). She also created a series for Showtime called *United States of Tara* (2009–), and she writes and hosts an online Web series called *Red Band Trailer*.

Spike Lee (1957–) has written and directed many films focusing on the experiences of African Americans in the United States. His script for the groundbreaking film *Do the Right Thing* (1989) was nominated for an Academy Award. He is known for his skillful use of dialogue. He has also directed and starred in a number of successful television commercials.

Frances Marion (1888–1973) was one of the most well-known screenwriters of the early 20th century. She won Academy Awards for her writing on *The Big House* (1930) and *The Champ* (1931), and wrote screenplays for actresses such as Mary Pickford, Marie Dressler, and Marion Davies.

Budd Schulberg (1914–2009) was a novelist, television producer, and screenwriter. Most famous for his Academy Award–winning screenplay for *On the Waterfront* (1954), he also wrote screenplays such as *A Face in the Crowd* (1957) and novels like *The Harder They Fall*.

GLOSSARY

conflict (KAHN-flikt) a problem that motivates characters in a story

dialogue (DIE-uh-lawg) conversation between two or more characters

directors (duh-REK-turz) people in charge of what we see happen in a movie, television show, or play

draft (DRAFT) a first version of a document or any version that is not final

drama (DRAH-muh) a serious play

extras (EK-struhz) actors who don't have any speaking lines and appear in the background in scenes

images (IM-ij-iz) visual representations of ideas

networking (NET-wurk-ing) meeting people to make business connections

plot (PLAHT) the events of a story

revised (ri-VIZED) to review and make changes

scene (SEEN) a small part of a larger story that takes place in a single location

screenwriters (SKREEN-rite-uhrz) a person who writes scripts for film or television

script (SKRIPT) written plan for a movie, TV show, or play

set (SET) the location where a show or movie is filmed

table read (TAY-buhl REED) rehearsal where actors read their speaking parts while sitting around a table

FOR MORE INFORMATION

BOOKS

Levine, Gail Carson. *Writing Magic: Creating Stories That Fly*. New York: Collins, 2006.

Loewen, Nancy, and Dawn Beacon (illustrator). *Action! Writing Your Own Play*. Mankato, MN: Picture Window Books, 2011.

Weinstein, Elizabeth, and Anna Dallam. *Shakespeare with Children: Six Scripts for Young Players*. Lyme, NH: Smith & Kraus, 2008.

WEB SITES

How Stuff Works—How Writing a TV Show Works
electronics.howstuffworks.com/tv-writing.htm
Information, pictures, and links about writing for television.

IMDb
www.imdb.com
Find out who wrote your favorite movies.

ZOOM Playhouse
pbskids.org/zoom/activities/playhouse
Read scripts and choose one to perform.

INDEX

ABOUT THE AUTHOR

Matt Mullins lives in Madison, Wisconsin, with his son and writes about science, engineering, business strategy, and other topics. Formerly a journalist, Matt has written more than 20 children's books, and has written and directed three short films.